A Break
in the Chain

Other titles in the bunch:

Amina's Blanket
A Break in the Chain
Colly's Barn
Deadly Friend
Dragon Trouble
Fine Feathered Friend

The Monster from Underground
My Brother Bernadette
Soccer Star
Storm
Stranger from Somewhere in Time
Who's a Clever Girl?

Crabtree Publishing Company
www.crabtreebooks.com

PMB 16A, 350 Fifth Avenue
Suite 3308
New York, NY 10118

612 Welland Avenue
St. Catharines, Ontario
Canada, L2M 5V6

D'Lacey, Chris
   A break in the chain / Chris d'Lacey ; illustrated by Joanna Carey.
   p. cm. -- (Yellow bananas)
   Summary: A terrible oil spill in the Arctic, a lesson about food chains, and a
computer game featuring a polar bear turn into a magical adventure for Billy, whose
class uses email and a fundraiser to help rescue the Arctic animals.
   ISBN 0-7787-0931-0 (RHB) -- ISBN 0-7787-0977-9 (pbk.)
   [1. Oil spills--Fiction. 2. Wildlife rescue--Fiction. 3. Food chains (Ecology)--
Fiction. 4. Computers--Fiction. 5. Schools --Fiction.]   I. Carey, Joanna, ill. II.
Title. III. Series.
PZ7.D6475Br 2003
[Fic]--dc21
                      2002009748
                      LC

Published by Crabtree Publishing in 2002
First published in Great Britain 1998 by Heinemann Young Books
imprints of Egmont Children's Books Limited
Text copyright © Chris d'Lacey 1998
Illustrations copyright © Joanna Carey 1998
The Author and Illustrator have asserted their moral rights.
Reinforced Hardcover Binding ISBN 0-7787-0931-0 Paperback ISBN 0-7787-0977-9

1 2 3 4 5 6 7 8 9 0 Printed in Italy 0 9 8 7 6 5 4 3 2

Chris d'Lacey

A Break
in the Chain

Illustrated by
JOANNA CAREY

 **YELLOW BANANAS**

For
Boley, Fizz and Sunshine

Chapter One

"TODAY," SAID MISS Harrison, "we're going to learn about the sorts of things that animals eat. In particular, we're going to find out about something called a food chain. What are we going to find out about, class?"

"A food chain!" the children shouted back.

"Good," said Miss Harrison. "Who can suggest an animal to start with?"

"A polar bear!" Tommy Fegan said.

"Very good," said Miss Harrison. "Do you know what polar bears eat, Tommy?"

Tommy shook his head.

"Never mind," said Miss Harrison, "let's ask our polar bear expert." She looked at Billy Ashcroft. Everybody knew that the polar bear was Billy's favorite animal.

"Billy, what do polar bears eat?"

Miss Harrison tapped her foot and waited for Billy to answer. But Billy was almost asleep. He'd stayed up late, playing his brand new CD-ROM the night before. It was called *The Frozen North* and it showed interesting things about the Arctic. If you clicked on the correct piece of snow or ice, a bear called Lorel popped out of his den and talked about the freezing Arctic climate.

Right at that moment, the climate was getting chilly in the classroom too. Miss Harrison was beginning to lose her patience.

"Wake up, Billy!" she said, clapping her hands.

Billy jumped in surprise. Miss Harrison frowned at him. "What are we learning, today?" she asked sternly.

Billy bit his lip. He didn't have a clue. He looked at his best friend, Josie Westacott. Josie tried to whisper something but Billy couldn't hear her properly.

"Food trains, Miss Harrison?" he tried.

The whole class snickered. Josie covered her face.

"Food chains," Miss Harrison said sternly. "We are trying to find out what a polar bear eats. Tonight, Mr. Sleepyhead, I would like you to find out something about the polar bear's food chain. You can tell the class all about it tomorrow."

"Yes, Miss Harrison," Billy mumbled.

Just then, the classroom door burst open. A chubby little man with a pencil behind

one ear staggered in carrying a large
cardboard box.

"Delivery," he puffed. "Where do you
want it?"

"On my desk, please," Miss Harrison beamed.

"What is it?" the children shouted.

The delivery man winked. He put the box
down and turned it around. Written across the
side was the word COMPUTER . . .

Chapter Two

"ANOTHER COMPUTER?" BILLY'S mom
said, as she put two bowls of spaghetti on
the table. "Goodness, you'll be going to the
moon next."

"It's great," said Josie, who had come over
for dinner. "It's got much better software than
the other computers. We're going to be on
the Internet. That means we can look up all
sorts of things."

"And send letters," Billy added, twirling a

strand of spaghetti around his fork.

"Letters?" said Mrs. Ashcroft doubtfully.

"You know, e-mail," Josie explained.

Mrs. Ashcroft hummed. "Well, I think I'll stick with good old-fashioned snail mail, the kind you put in a mailbox, thank you. Internet, indeed. You'll be telling me it makes dinner next."

"It's got a CD-ROM drive," Billy said excitedly, "so I'll be able to take *The Frozen North* to school." That reminded him – about Miss Harrison's assignment.

"Mom," he said, "what's a food chain?"

"One with polar bears in it," Josie added.

"A food chain?" Mrs. Ashcroft repeated. "It's a group of supermarkets, isn't it?"

Josie wrinkled her nose. "I don't think so," she muttered, looking at Billy. "I've never seen a bear in a supermarket, have you?"

Just then, Billy's dad
walked in. He said
hello to Josie, gave
his wife a kiss,
tousled Billy's hair
and switched the TV
on. Mr. Ashcroft liked
to watch the evening
news while he was
eating his dinner.

"What's a food
chain, Dad?" Billy
asked again.

Mr. Ashcroft
grinned. "It's what
you get if you tie
some spaghetti
together."

Billy and Josie
laughed. Mrs. Ashcroft
didn't. Something on
the TV had caught
her eye.

"Ooh," she said, "a polar bear."

"Where?" said Billy, turning to look.

Sure enough, there on the TV news was a polar bear. It was pacing restlessly across the ice, shaking its paws as if it was trying to throw something off. Billy frowned and leaned in closer to the set. The polar bear's paws were a funny color. So was the ice it was walking on. So were all the animals lying on the ice. Billy recognized them now. They were Arctic Seals. Seals, he knew, were normally grayish-white. But these seals were black, slimy jet black.

Suddenly, the TV picture changed.

It showed an oil tanker far out in the ocean. The ship was broken and lurching on its side. Oil was spilling from a hole in its hull. Huge sheets of oil were spreading across the ocean and lapping ashore. Then Billy realized what was wrong – the ice and the animals were covered in oil.

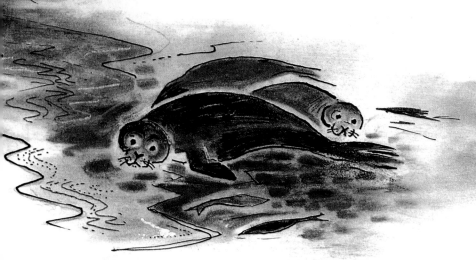

"This is the worst environmental disaster the Arctic has ever seen," said a newscaster. "The cost of cleaning up the oil is estimated at many millions of dollars. The cost to local wildlife is already very much higher than that."

Josie shuddered and turned her face away
as the TV showed evidence of dead sea birds,
drenched in oil. Even Mr. Ashcroft gulped
uneasily. Just then, the newscaster said:
"Experts fear that the Arctic food chain could
be broken . . ."

"What?" cried Billy.

"Come on," said Mr. Ashcroft, patting Billy's
arm, "finish your supper. There's
nothing you can do."

Billy frowned. There ought
to be something he could do
for those animals. He sadly
twirled some spaghetti
around his fork, ate one
more mouthful then
pushed his
plate away.
Suddenly, he didn't
feel hungry any more.

Chapter Three

WHEN JOSIE HAD left, Billy went upstairs
to play *The Frozen North*. He was hoping to
learn about the polar bear's food chain, but
somehow he couldn't concentrate. He clicked
wearily around the screen and even yawned
a couple of times. Soon, he abandoned
the computer altogether and trudged
downstairs to get a drink of water. But he
couldn't stop thinking about the bear and the
oil. What had the newscaster meant when
he'd said: "The Arctic food chain could be
broken?" Billy sighed and went to sit in the

backyard. He wished someone could explain it to him.

Just then, something peculiar happened: a few snowflakes started to fall and the air turned very misty and cold. Billy lifted his glass to take a drink of water . . . only to find his water had frozen! The next thing he knew there was ice all around him. Suddenly, something came out of the mist. Something large and white with rounded ears and a big black nose. Great puffs of polar breath were blowing from its jaws. It was Lorel, the bear from *The Frozen North!*

"It's you!" cried Billy.

"Is it?" said Lorel.

"Yes," Billy nodded. "How did you get here?"

"Don't know," said the bear.

"It doesn't matter," said Billy. "Have *you* come to tell me about food chains and the oil?"

"Probably," said the bear, looking a bit confused. "Is that what this smelly black stuff is?" He lifted up a paw. It was covered in oil.

"Yes," said Billy, having a sniff.

"I don't suppose you know how to get it off?"

Billy thought he did. "Hang on," he said.

"What to?" asked Lorel, looking around.

But Billy had already dashed into the kitchen. He had often seen his dad scrub oil off his hands. He used soap and a stiff nailbrush. Billy didn't think a nailbrush would

16

be much use on a polar bear. So he ran to the garage for the big broom instead. Then he squirted some soap into a pail and filled it up with water. He carried the bucket and the broom outside.

"Lie down," said Billy. Lorel flopped onto his stomach. Billy dipped the broom in the soapy water and started scrubbing Lorel's fur!

Soon the oil began to come off. Billy had to scrub hard, but Lorel didn't mind. He seemed to be enjoying every minute of it!

"Left a bit," he said, wiggling his behind. "Up a bit. Stop. There! Scrub there!"

"Besides being so messy," Billy puffed, "what's so bad about all that oil?"

The bear rolled on his back with his paws in the air. "It sticks to your fur when you swim in it," he said, "and if you try to lick it off, it makes you sick! The fish don't like it; it poisons them. And if the seals eat the fish, it poisons them, too! Do you think you could scrub my stomach now?"

Billy sighed and clambered up the bear's side. "So, will someone scrub the fish clean?" he said. That would be difficult. Even with a nail brush.

"No," said the bear. "The fish will die."

"But if they die," said Billy, "the seals won't have any good fish to eat – then they'll die."

"I know," said the bear, his great stomach rumbling, "and then we won't have any seals to eat."

"But then you'll die, too!" Billy exclaimed.

"Yes," said the bear. "I think you missed a bit under my chin."

Billy did the bear's chin and jumped down quickly. "This is terrible," he said. "I'm going to tell Miss Harrison about it."

"Good idea," said the bear. "Tell everyone you know."

"I will," Billy said. "I might write to my congress person – that's what Dad always says we should do. I might send a letter on the school computer!"

"Good idea," said the bear, though he hadn't the foggiest idea what a congressperson, a letter, or a computer were.

"If you're hungry now, I could run and ask Mom to cook you something?" Billy said.

"Seal?" said the bear, with a hopeful look.

Billy shook his head. "I think seals are too big to fit in the freezer. We've got fish sticks! I can get you some of those!" And he ran into the kitchen to have a look.

That was where his mom caught up with him. "Billy," she said, tapping his shoulder, "what are you doing? Close that fridge."

"I'm getting some food for the bear!" explained Billy.

Mrs. Ashcroft looked puzzled. "Bear? What bear?"

Billy pointed to the backyard – but other than the faintest dusting of snow, Lorel and the ice had completely disappeared.

"Come on," said Mrs. Ashcroft, "upstairs to bed – and don't forget to turn that computer off, please."

Billy scratched his head. He was sure he'd seen a bear. It had told him things about the food chain, hadn't it? He trudged upstairs a bit confused. On the computer, his snowflake screensaver had started up. He nudged the mouse and a scene from *The Frozen North* appeared. It was Lorel, the polar bear, sitting there, waiting. Billy clicked on Lorel's nose.

"Don't forget what I told you," Lorel whispered – and the program shut down.

Chapter Four

AT SCHOOL THE next day, everyone was talking about the oil spill.

"Calm down, class," Miss Harrison said. "We *will* do something to help the animals." She turned to Billy: "You did a good job researching the food chain, Billy. Your CD-ROM sounds very interesting. It's quite useful, being able to talk to a bear! He seems to have told you a lot about the food chain."

The class began to giggle. Miss Harrison smiled. She turned to the board and drew four pictures – some tiny things called plankton, a fish, a seal, and a tubby polar bear.

"This is the polar bear's food chain," she said, drawing a line between each picture. "The bears survive by eating the seals, the seals eat the fish, and the fish eat the plankton. But if an accident causes even the plankton to die, it can affect all the other animals higher up the chain."

She rubbed out the fish and drew a sad face on the seal. Then she rubbed out the seal and drew an even sadder face on the bear.

"An oil spill can make this happen. We say it breaks the chain."

"But, what can we do?" asked Josie.

"Two things," said Miss Harrison. "First, we can write to the leaders of the oil-producing nations and tell them how concerned we are about the effect oil spills have on the environment. Secondly, we can raise some money to send to the Arctic Wildlife Appeal!"

The children cheered. Billy raised his hand.

"How are we going to do it, Miss Harrison?"

"Ah," said Miss Harrison, "your polar bear has given me an idea . . ."

Chapter Five

"A SPONSORED SCRUB!" Mrs. Ashcroft laughed. "That'll be the day! I have to chase you into the bath as it is!"

"Not *us*, Mom," said Billy. "We're scrubbing a rug."

"A rug?" said Mrs. Ashcroft. "What for?"

"It's a white one," said Josie, "like a polar bear's fur. Miss Harrison's going to spill oil all over it and we're going to scrub it off – 50 cents for five minutes. Will you sponsor me, please? You have to sign this piece of paper."

"Me too," said Billy, "I'm going to do an hour!"

Mrs. Ashcroft scratched her head. "Well, it's an odd way to raise money. Still, it is a good cause. Brian, sponsor them!"

"What?" said Mr. Ashcroft, nearly choking on his coffee. Billy pushed the sponsor form under his dad's nose.

"It's for the polar bears, Dad. We can save them if we send money quickly to help clean the oil from their fur."

Mr. Ashcroft winced. "Can't you write a letter to your congressperson instead?"

"We're doing that as well," beamed Josie.
"And we're writing to all the oil-producing
nations of the world."

"On the new computer," Billy said.

Mrs. Ashcroft nodded at her husband.
"There," she said proudly, "the new computer."

"All right, put me down for five dollars,"
Mr. Ashcroft sighed.

Chapter Six

THE SPONSORED SCRUB was a huge success.
Josie got twelve sponsors; Billy got eleven.
He asked everyone he knew, including the
garbage collector, the postal carrier, and the
girl who delivered their paper. Even Mr.
Gribble, Billy's grumpy next door neighbor,
signed up for two whole dollars worth of
scrubbing – but only on the understanding
that Billy would wash his car as well.

The scrub was held on a Saturday morning.
All the parents came to watch. A reporter
from the Ruffley Gazette also came. She
took pictures of the children holding scrub
brushes in one hand and buckets in the other!
Billy thought he saw a man with a video
camera, but he didn't pay much attention
to it.

At ten o'clock precisely, Miss Harrison
uncurled the rug in the schoolyard. Mr
Creekmore, the principal, splashed it with oil.
Everyone shouted, "Boo!" Miss Harrison put a
whistle to her lips.

"Ready?" she shouted. The children cheered.
Miss Harrison blew – and the scrubbing
began!

It was very hard work – worse than scrubbing a bear, Billy thought. By the time Miss Harrison blew the whistle again, he felt as if his arms were about to fall off. Mr. Creekmore got a hose and washed the soap suds away. The parents clapped, but most of the children had very long faces. There were still a lot of oily patches on the rug.

Oddly enough, Miss Harrison seemed pleased. She turned the children to face their parents. "Thank you for sponsoring our scrubbers!" she said. "Please note, despite their hard work, the rug is still oily. This is to

show just how difficult it can be to clean up an oil spill! Imagine this as a polar bear's fur!"

The parents looked impressed.

"So!" Miss Harrison announced firmly. "We are now going to write to all the oil-producing countries to express our concern, aren't we class?"

"Yes!" they chorused – and rushed into the classroom.

Everyone wanted to be first to the computer – to watch Miss Harrison type the message!

Chapter Seven

"THIS COMPUTER," MISS Harrison said, with twenty-six goggled-eyed children around her, "is able to send electronic messages to other computers all over the world. First we have to type an address – like this:"

president@whitehouse.usa

"The White House is where the President lives; gov stands for government. The funny squiggle means "at". So we're sending our message to the President at his home in the White House."

"Are we really writing to Washington?" gasped Josie.

"Not just Washington," Miss Harrison stressed. "We'll be sending the same letter to the governments of all the countries that transport oil. This is just an example. Watch!"

Dear Mr President, Miss Harrison typed, **The staff and children of Ruffley Public School, wish to express their deep concern about the oil spill in the Arctic. We are shocked at the sight of polluted coastlines and the suffering inflicted on local wildlife. We would like your assurance that our government will be doing everything in its power to prevent such a disaster from ever happening again, in the hope that future generations will still have some wildlife left to enjoy.**
Yours sincerely,
Miss Julia Harrison (teacher)

"Ready?" said Miss Harrison.

The children nodded. Miss Harrison clicked the mouse. The computer beeped.

Message sent, it reported. And everyone cheered.

On Monday morning, the first replies arrived. The new computer beeped three times during Miss Harrison's talk on recycling. The children could barely contain their excitement.

"Slowly!" she thundered, when she finally allowed them up to her desk. When everyone was settled, Miss Harrison clicked on the e-mail folder. The children gasped as a message flashed. It said:

Thank you for mailing the Kremlin. The Russian President has been informed of your comments.

"Is that it?" said Josie. A groan of disappointment echoed around the class – especially since the replies from Kuwait and Canada said almost the same thing.

Miss Harrison sighed. "World leaders are very busy people," she said. "We can't expect too much, too soon. Besides, we did raise three hundred and seventy two dollars from our sponsored scrub. That's going to help save some animals, isn't it? I thought we might also e-mail other schools and tell them about our scrub-a-rug idea to see if they want to try it themselves."

Everyone thought that was a great idea, and the computer was beeping like mad all

afternoon as e-mail messages whizzed back and forth. Everyone in the class were really enjoying themselves. No one wanted school to finish that day, until Miss Harrison mysteriously announced:

"One last thing. I want you all to watch the local evening news tonight. You might see something very interesting . . ."

When Billy's dad came home that night the TV set was already on. Billy was watching a news report, all about the Arctic Wildlife Appeal. It showed sea birds having their feathers cleaned, then being released far away from the oil.

"It is a mammoth task," the reporter was saying, "and the clean-up will continue for

many months yet. But thanks to the efforts of local children, like these at Ruffley Public School, countless lives have already been saved." Suddenly, the TV picture changed and Billy almost fell off his seat. His class was on television – doing their sponsored scrub!

"Looks fun, doesn't it?" the reporter chuckled. "This big guy certainly isn't complaining . . ."

Billy bit his lip. His eyes went very moist.
On the screen now was a real polar bear. He
was lying on the ice, fast asleep it seemed,
while a man scrubbed the oil off his fur. Now
Billy knew that he and his class really had
done something to help the animals –
something good, something special,
something almost magical.

And the magic didn't end there.

Later that night, Billy went upstairs to play *The Frozen North*. The computer was on and the snowflake screensaver had started up. Billy sat down and nudged the mouse. The snowflake pattern didn't disappear. Billy tapped the keyboard. Still the snowflakes tumbled down. Billy sighed and was just about to call his dad, when the snowflakes began to form a message:

**Well done, Billy
we're proud of you!**

and underneath was the sender's e-mail address

Lorel@frozen.north

 YELLOW BANANAS

Don't forget there's a whole bunch of Yellow Bananas to choose from:

Amina's Blanket
A Break in the Chain
Colly's Barn
Dragon Trouble
Fine Feathered Friend
Jo-Jo the Melon Donkey
The Monster from Underground
My Brother Bernadette
Soccer Star
Storm
Stranger from Somewhere in Time
Who's a Clever Girl?